IVA DUNNIT and the BIG WIND

Hutchinson

London   Melbourne   Auckland   Johannesburg

IVA DUNNIT
and the BIG WIND

by CAROL PURDY

Pictures by STEVEN KELLOGG

First published by William Morrow Inc, New York 1985
First published in Great Britain 1987 by Hutchinson Children's Books
An imprint of Century Hutchinson Ltd
Brookmount House, 62–65 Chandos Place, Covent Garden
London WC2N 4NW

Century Hutchinson Australia (Pty) Ltd
16–22 Church Street, Hawthorn, Melbourne, Victoria 3122

Century Hutchinson New Zealand Ltd
32–34 View Road, PO Box 40–086, Glenfield, Auckland 10

Century Hutchinson South Africa (Pty) Ltd
PO Box 337, Bergvlei 2012, South Africa

This edition by arrangement with Sheldon Fogelman
Printed in Great Britain by Scotprint Ltd, Musselburgh
and bound by Hunter and Foulis Ltd, Edinburgh

British Library Cataloguing in Publication Data
Purdy, Carol
  Iva Dunnit and the big wind.
  I. Title II. Kellogg, Steven
  813'.54[J]   PZ7

  ISBN 0-09-172679-4

To John
C. P.

For Helen and those six fine children
with appreciation and love
S. K.

ack in the days of petticoats and wagon trails there was a pioneer woman named Iva Dunnit. She had six fine children – Ida and Ivan, Ima and Isaac, Ira and Little Iris. They lived on a homestead near the town of Cob Hollow.

Folks in Cob Hollow wondered how a woman with six children could survive alone on the prairie. But that didn't bother Iva Dunnit. She always said, 'There's only three things we need – our wits, our strength, and young'uns that knows how to stay put.'

Iva Dunnit wasn't afraid of anything, and she and her six fine children could handle most troubles that came their way. Once they fought off a prairie fire.

'My young'uns stayed put and done like I told them,' bragged Iva Dunnit.

Once they saved Little Iris from a pack of wolves.

'With our strength we can lick a pack of wolves any day,' said Iva Dunnit.

And once Iva Dunnit and Isaac outwitted a thief who came to steal their horses. 'I reckon Isaac inherited my wits,' Iva Dunnit told the folks in Cob Hollow.

But this story is about the time Iva Dunnit herself got stuck out in the Big Wind.

Every summer around Cob Hollow there came a spell of bad weather folks called the Big Wind. It was a wind so fierce folks didn't often venture out while it was raging. Why once the Big Wind blew old Doc Fenton clean to the next town, and through the glass door of the barber's shop.

Old Doc Fenton was right famous for his scrapes with the Big Wind.

Well, one hot afternoon in August the Big Wind started up and Iva Dunnit rushed her children into the house. 'I feel plumb cosy,' said Iva Dunnit. 'Sure glad I got you six fine young'uns to snuggle up with while the wind's a blowin'.'

'Sure glad we got this tight house to keep out the Big Wind,' said Isaac.

'Yes sirree,' said Iva Dunnit. 'And a tight barn to shelter them chickens so we can keep right on collectin' their eggs for provisions.'

'How do you know them chickens is *in* the barn?' said Ida. 'There ain't no critter dumber than a chicken.'

Right then Iva Dunnit quit feeling so cosy. 'I got to check them hens,' she said. 'If we lose our livin', you young'uns will get mighty hungry long about time the beans run out.'

Iva Dunnit's skirt and petticoats made a sail, and she got to the barn sooner than she expected. 'We'll help, Ma,' said Isaac.

Iva Dunnit couldn't believe her ears. 'Didn't I tell you young'uns to stay put?' she cried.

'No, Ma. You didn't say nothin' about stayin' put,' said Ida. 'We come to help save our livin'.'

'Y'all get in the house directly,' yelled Iva Dunnit, 'And this time *stay put!*'

Sure enough, four of the best hens were missing. 'Blame it all,' said Iva Dunnit. 'I reckon they'll be scattered all over.'

Right away she spotted the chickens, but her petticoats kept sailing her back to the barn. 'Reckon there's only one answer,' said Iva Dunnit, stooping to wriggle out of her skirts. 'I'spect some old homesteader will be surprised to find them petticoats in his barnyard.'

Just then Iva Dunnit glanced toward the house and saw an awful sight. A flap of roofing had blown loose. 'I'll just hold down the roof while I call those young'uns to bring a hammer,' she said.

Soon as Iva Dunnit got there, she realized she couldn't hold down the roof with two chickens in each hand. But it took more than that to stop Iva Dunnit. 'Good hens,' she said as she tied the chickens to her corset strings.

Just as she managed to pull the roofing into place, the Big Wind snatched the ladder.

Iva Dunnit hollered till her throat ached. Her hands were numb and her arms felt near to breaking. But the Big Wind blew away her voice and no one came.

After a long spell Iva Dunnit said, 'Why haven't them young'uns come to see what happened to their ma? I'll be 'bliged to tell them a thing or two when I get down from here.'

More time passed, and Iva Dunnit was entering a dream world. She closed her eyes and had a new thought. 'Why, them young'uns can't come lookin' for me 'cause I told them to stay put. Yes sirree, if there's one thing I pride myself on it's havin' young'uns that knows how to *stay put*.'

Iva Dunnit felt happy. She grabbed a passing chicken by its corset strings and told it, 'If I die hangin' here in my drawers, those young'uns'll never know. They'll spend the rest of their days stayin' put like I told them.'

But the truth is Iva Dunnit's children were finally beginning to wonder what had happened to their ma.

The sharp bing, bang, bam of a hammer jarred Iva Dunnit back into real life.

'Hang on, Ma,' said Isaac. 'We'll have you down directly.'

Ivan grabbed Iva Dunnit by the waist. 'Let go,' he hollered.

'How'd you know to come lookin' for me?' asked Iva Dunnit.

'Ma, you've taught us to use our wits,' said Ivan. 'When it took a mighty age for you to come back, we figured it was better to go find you than to stay put.'

'Bless your heart, Ivan,' said Iva Dunnit. 'I'd have dropped soon, and we'd have lost our roof sure.'

Tucked safely in bed, Iva Dunnit felt like a queen. Ima popped corn that filled the house with a delicious toasty smell, while Ivan and Isaac told how they had found Ma dangling from the roof in her drawers with four chickens tied to her corset strings.

'Boy, howdy!' said Ira. 'Ma, Isaac and Ivan done saved our house and our livin' from the Big Wind.'

Iva Dunnit sighed and said, 'It's a mighty grand feelin' to have your wits and strength. But the best thing I have is young'uns that knows when to stay put *and* when to go lookin' for their ma.'

'Listen,' said Little Iris. 'It sounds like the Big Wind done quit.'